A TOON BOOK BY

R. KIKUO JOHNSON

ASIAN/PACIFIC AMERICAN AWARD FOR LITERATURE
ALSC'S GRAPHIC NOVELS READING LIST
HARVEY AWARD NOMINEE
A JUNIOR LIBRARY GUILD SELECTION

For Danielle

Editorial Director: FRANÇOISE MOULY

Book Design: FRANÇOISE MOULY & JONATHAN BENNETT

R. KIKUO JOHNSON'S artwork was drawn in ink and colored digitally.

All our books are Smyth Sewn (the highest library-quality binding available) and printed with soy-based inks on acid-free woodfree paper harvested from responsible sources. Printed in Dongguan, China, by Toppan Leefung. Distributed to the trade by Consortium Book Sales and Distribution, Inc.; orders (800) 283-3572; orderentry@perseusbooks.com; www.cbsd.com.

The Library of Congress has cataloged the hardcover edition as follows:

Johnson, R. Kikuo. The Shark King : A TOON book / by R. Kikuo Johnson. p. cm. Summary: In graphic novel format, retells the Hawaiian story of Nanaue, born of human mother and shark father, who struggles to find his place in a village of humans. ISBN 978-1-935179-16-0 (hardcover) 1. Graphic novels. [1. Graphic novels. 2. Folklore--Hawaii.] I. Title.

PZ7.7.J642Sh 2012 741.5'973--dc23 2011026592

ISBN: 978-1-935179-16-0 (hardcover)

ISBN: 978-1-935179-60-3 (paperback)

17 18 19 20 21 22 TPN 10 9 8 7 6 5 4 3

www.TOON-BOOKS.com

Chapter 1
LONG AGO IN HAWAII, A YOUNG WOMAN NAMED KALEI
WAS SEARCHING FOR HER FAVORITE FOOD...

AHA!
OPIHI:* A DELICIOUS SEA SNAIL
*oh-PEE-hee
SUDDENLY...

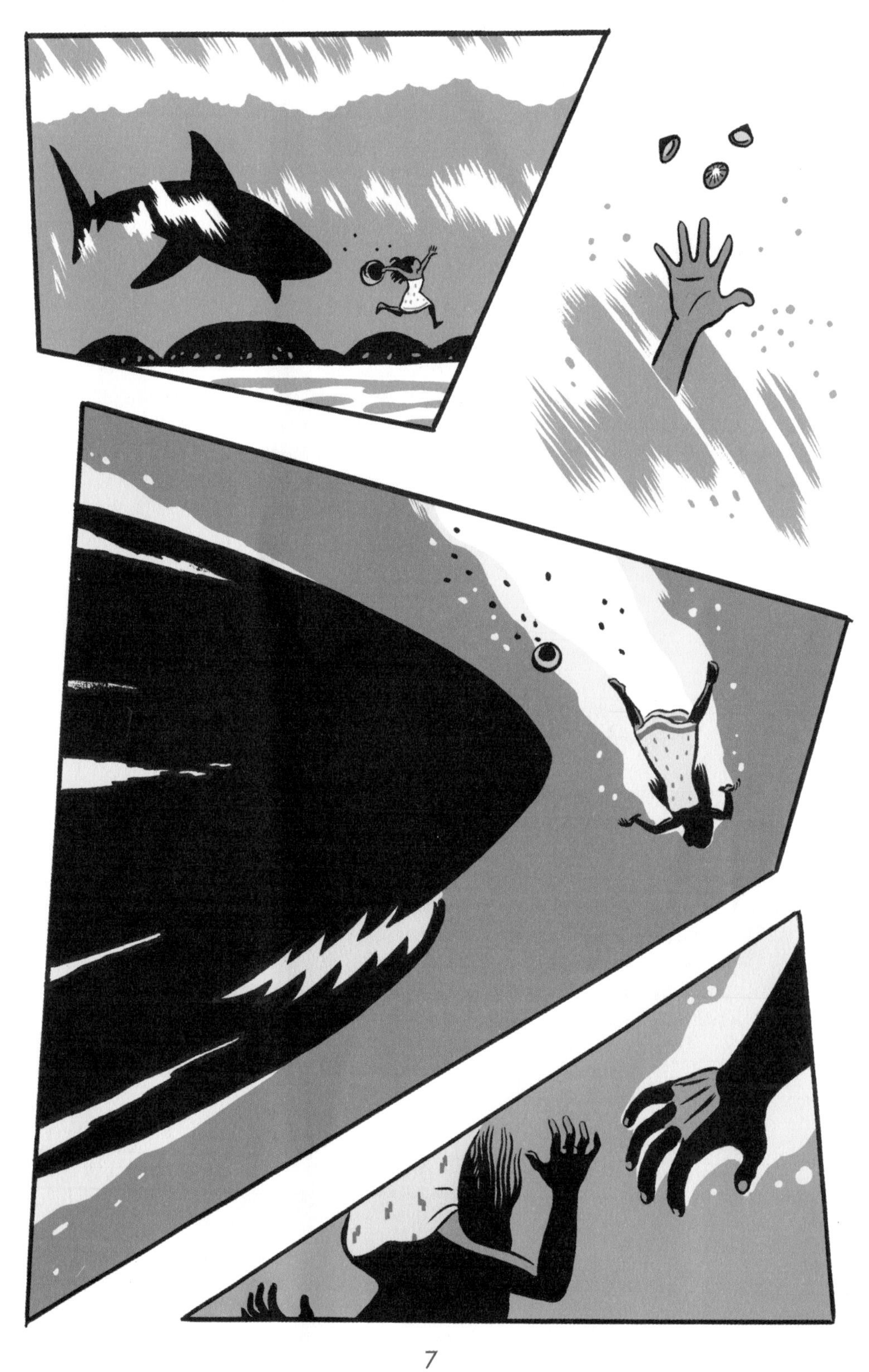

COUGH
COUGH

Thank you- I thought I was alone...

Is this your first time here?
Yes...

The King doesn't like *strangers*.
KING? What king?

The SHARK KING, of course! He can change into any creature large or small...

...He could have swallowed you whole!
GROWL
He must not be as hungry as I am... I wish I hadn't lost all my opihi!

Where did you get those?
These opihi?

The sea is full of surprises today.

IN TIME, KALEI AND HER RESCUER FELL DEEPLY IN LOVE.

Will you marry me?

YES!

ONE DAY...

SPLASH

He's been down there for *hours!*

I thought the Shark King had *eaten* you!
HA HA! No, my love...

...I'm making a place for our son at the bottom of the pool.

BUT THE NIGHT BEFORE THE CHILD WAS BORN...
I'm leaving...

Where are you going?
Our son won't be safe in this world. I'm going where I can *protect* him.

Here. He'll need this.
Your *cape?*

WAIT!
His skin feels *rough!*
GILLS?
...FINS?!

He's the SHARK KING!

Chapter 2
KALEI'S SON WAS BORN LAUGHING.
HA HA!
I'll call you NANAUE!*

*nah-NOW-way

SOON, NANAUE TOOK HIS FIRST STEPS...
You're walking!

MORE!
You're *talking*!

BUT AS HE GREW...
This *mark* is getting bigger and bigger...

SNAP
SNAP

AND SO...
Put this cape on!
NO! *HA HA!*

Someone might see you!
HA HA HA!

SPLASH

No fish in the sea can outswim ME!

AND SO...
He's been down there all day...

SUDDENLY...
Strangers!

NANAUE!

Someone's coming!

Hurry up and put this on!
HI!

HI! Do you want to come fishing with me and my dad?
YES!

SNAP
SNAP

Whoops! Come to think of it, I *can't*... Maybe another time?
Maybe NOT!

>sigh.<

You did the *right thing*, Nanaue.

Can I go for a swim?
Sure.

BUT NANAUE FOLLOWS THE STRANGERS...

WOW! Look at all the fish, Dad!

That's how you throw a fishnet, son!
SPLASH

PULL!
HA HA!

Empty!
But there were so many fish!

Look, Ma!

THAT NIGHT...
Where did you learn how to fish?
It's easy!

LATER...
Bedtime!

Nanaue?

Where's *my* dad?

I don't know, honey...

...but I know *wherever* he is, he can't wait to meet you.

THE NEXT DAY...
They came back!

There they are! Look at all the fish!

SPLASH

Fishermen *know* where the fish are!

NOTHING!

AND EACH NIGHT, NANAUE SURPRISED HIS MOTHER WITH A BIGGER CATCH...
MONDAY.
TUESDAY.
WEDNESDAY.
THURSDAY.
FRIDAY.
BUT...
BURP!
I'm still HUNGRY!

SO EACH DAY, NANAUE FOLLOWED THE FISHERMEN FARTHER AND FARTHER FROM HIS HOME...

UNTIL ONE DAY...
A *village!*

SPLASH

Chapter 3
We haven't caught anything in weeks!
I'm so hungry!
We all are, son...

It's like something is *eating* the fish right off our *hooks!*

HEY! You're that *weird kid!*
Oh... hi!

SNAP
SNAP

A MONSTER!
SNAP SNAP
HE'S the one stealing our FOOD!

SMACK
SMACK
STOP HIM!

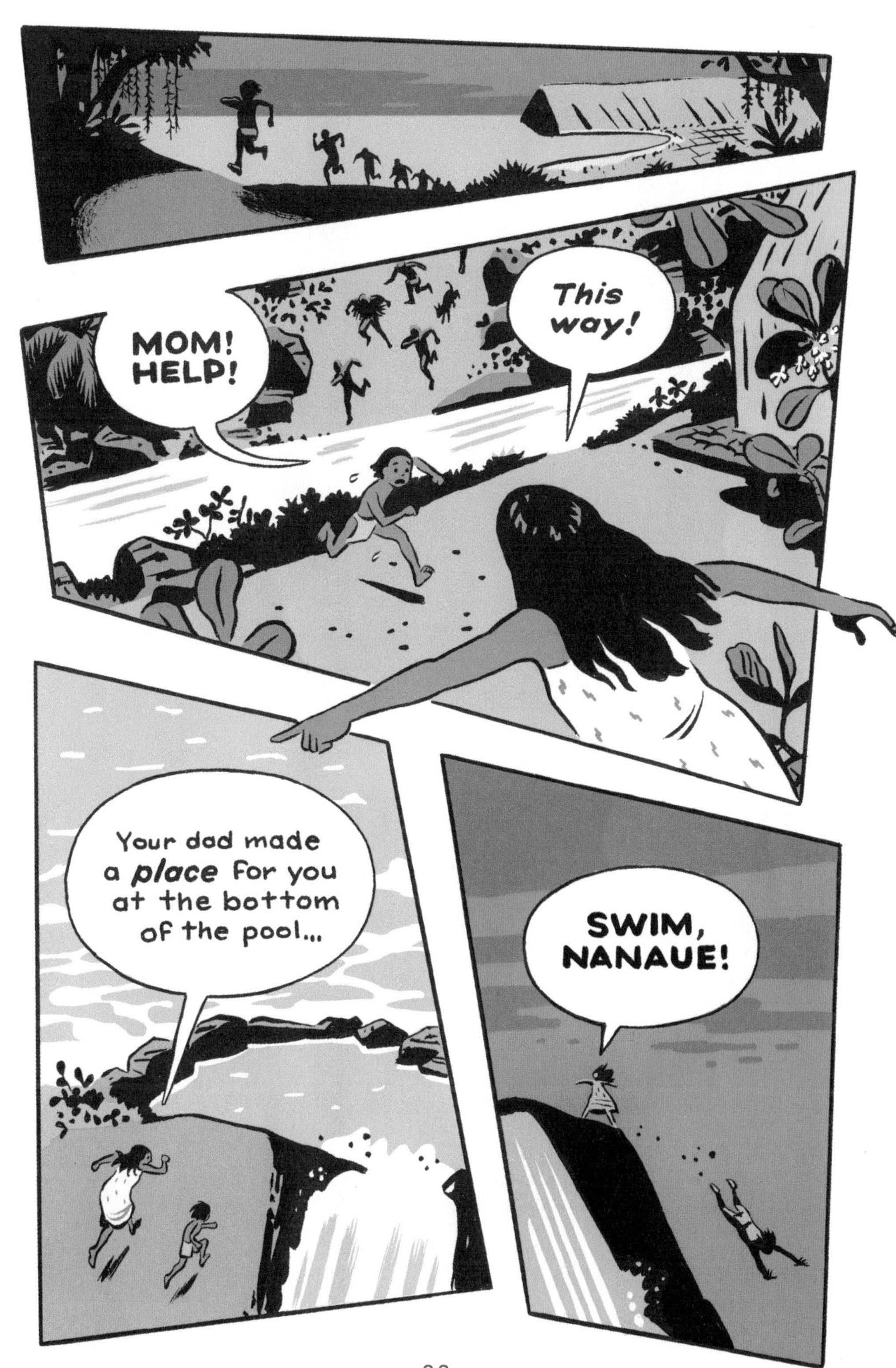
MOM! HELP!
This way!
Your dad made a *place* for you at the bottom of the pool...
SWIM, NANAUE!

SPLASH
He's *trapped!*
Fill the pool with *stones!*

MEANWHILE...
There!
A tunnel to the outside!
SOON...

BACK AT THE VILLAGE ...
PULL!

So many *fish!*
Let the feast begin!

TIME PASSED...

AND ONE DAY...

The *cape!*

You're with me always, my ***shark kings...***

the End

ABOUT THE AUTHOR

R. KIKUO JOHNSON grew up in Hawaii on the island of Maui. For generations, native Hawaiians have told tales of the shape-shifting shark god, Kamohoalii; *The Shark King* is the artist's version of one such tale about the insatiable appetite of Kamohoalii's son, Nanaue. Kikuo's 2005 graphic novel, *Night Fisher*—also set in Hawaii—earned him both the Russ Manning Most Promising Newcomer Award and a Harvey Award. Kikuo spent his childhood exploring the rocky shore in front of his grandmother's house at low tide and diving with his older brother. Since moving to the mainland, Kikuo has discovered the joys of swimming in fresh water and currently lives in Brooklyn, New York, where he enjoys cooking, playing his ukulele, and riding his bike all over the city.

HOW TO "TOON INTO READING"

in a few simple steps:

Our goal is to get kids reading—and we know kids LOVE comics. We publish award-winning early readers in comics form for elementary and early middle school, and present them in three levels.

FIND THE RIGHT BOOK

Veteran teacher Cindy Rosado tells what makes a good book for beginning and struggling readers alike: "A vetted vocabulary, plenty of picture clues, repetition, and a clear and compelling story. Also, the book shouldn't be too easy—or the reader won't learn, but neither should it be too hard—or he or she may get discouraged."

The TOON INTO READING!™ program is designed for beginning readers and works wonders with reluctant readers.

TAKE TIME WITH SILENT PANELS

Comics use panels to mark time, and silent panels count. Look and "read" even when there are no words. Often, humor is all in the timing!

GUIDE YOUNG READERS

What works?

Keep your fingertip below the character that is speaking.

LET THE PICTURES TELL THE STORY

In a comic, you can often read the story even if you don't know all the words. Encourage young readers to tell you what's happening based on the facial expressions and body language.

GET OUT THE CRAYONS

Kids see the hand of the author in a comic and it makes them want to tell their own stories. Encourage them to talk, write and draw!

Get kids talking, and you'll be surprised at how perceptive they are about pictures.

LET THEM GUESS

Comics provide a large amount of context for the words, so let young readers make informed guesses, and don't over-correct. In this panel, the artist shows a pirate ship, two pirate hats, and two pirate flags the first time the word "PIRATE" is introduced.